WITHDRAWN

PANCHO BANDITO

and the Amarillo Armadillo

Written by Mike Sundy

Illustrated by Jonathan Sundy

Pancho Bandito didn't start off tough. He was born with a smile sweeter than fresh horchata.

But the Old West was tryin'
on a boy and he had to learn
to fend for himself.

Pancho grew up a natural on the range. He made a rattlesnake lasso, spoke all twenty-seven dialects of coyote, and could herd more cattle 'n twenty men.

But there was one lack in his cowboyin' skills that really gnawed at him. Sure as shootin', he tried to ride horses but they turned out more like horse flapjacks.

He saw other cowboys on their trusty steeds and goldurned if it didn't leave him forlorn.

'Bout the only thing what could turn his frown upside-down was his favorite snack: Hatch chiles.

One day, Pancho drove his cattle across the Texas border to the Fort Worth Stockyards.

He haggled with an old rancher for a fair price. They were about to shake when a rumble of thunder split the prairie.

"These Texans ain't got no kind of
backbone what be scared of a puny armadillo.
Why, I can't even see 'im over yonder mountain range."

But there ain't no mountains in Fort Worth. The Amarillo Armadillo roared to life.

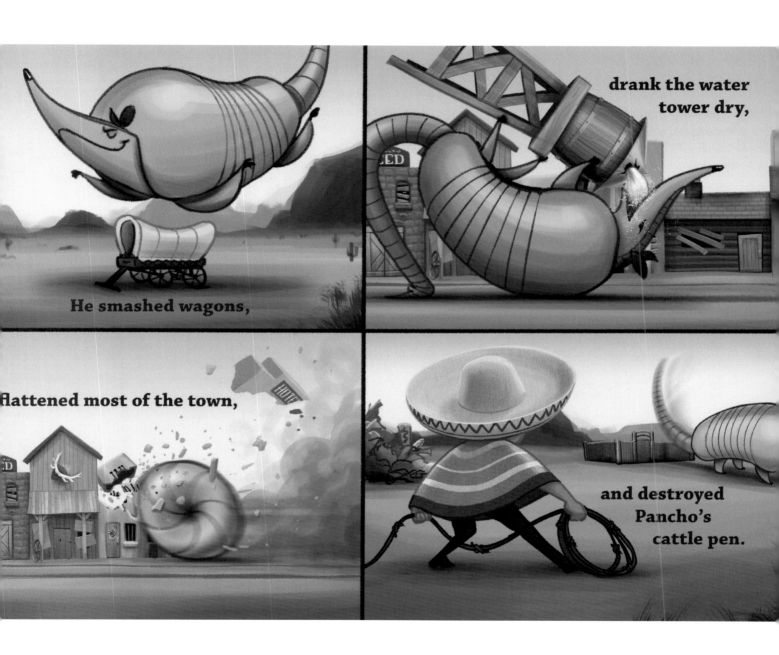

He smashed wagons,

drank the water tower dry,

flattened most of the town,

and destroyed Pancho's cattle pen.

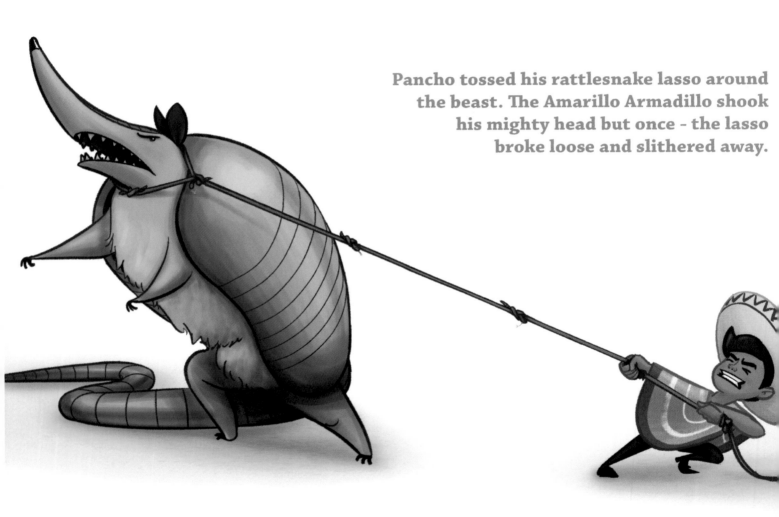

Pancho tossed his rattlesnake lasso around the beast. The Amarillo Armadillo shook his mighty head but once - the lasso broke loose and slithered away.

This made Pancho do his famous squint, the kind of squint that makes a charging buffalo stop dead in its tracks.

That riled Pancho right up -
he grabbed the monster and
they wrassled through the hills.

Pancho could tell that wrasslin' alone would not bring down the beast. So he jumped on AA's back to tame him.

But Pancho
slipped right off
them armor-plated
scales like butter in a skillet.

So he hopped
onto AA's snout
and held tight.

The Amarillo Armadillo bucked and whinnied and moved all tarnation until he shot Pancho up to the edge of the vast Texas sky.

Between the bucking and the
fighting, AA was tuckered out.

AA yawned and rolled over.
His snout wiggled until it
found Pancho's saddlebag.

SNIFF!

SNIFF!

AA looked up with puppy dog eyes. Pancho was a tough kid but somethin' 'bout this creature reminded him of when he was a baby.

Pancho and AA set about repairing the town,
which didn't take long on account of their size.

Well, reckon I should round up my cattle. A cowboy belongs on the range.

Mike Sundy
Author

Mike writes children's books and screenplays in the San Francisco Bay area. He's a graduate of the University of Notre Dame, currently works at Pixar Animation Studios, and wrassles bears for sport.

phastman@hotmail.com
mikesundy.blogspot.com

Jonathan Sundy
Illustrator

Jonathan is a freelance character designer and illustrator living in Portland. He attended Notre Dame and was the Design Director at Metaphase Design Group before moving to Oregon to focus on drawing silly things.

jsundy@gmail.com
jonathansundy.com

CPSIA information can be obtained at www.ICGtesting.com
Printed in the USA
LVIW01n1434200417
531553LV00007B/57

9 781517 362621